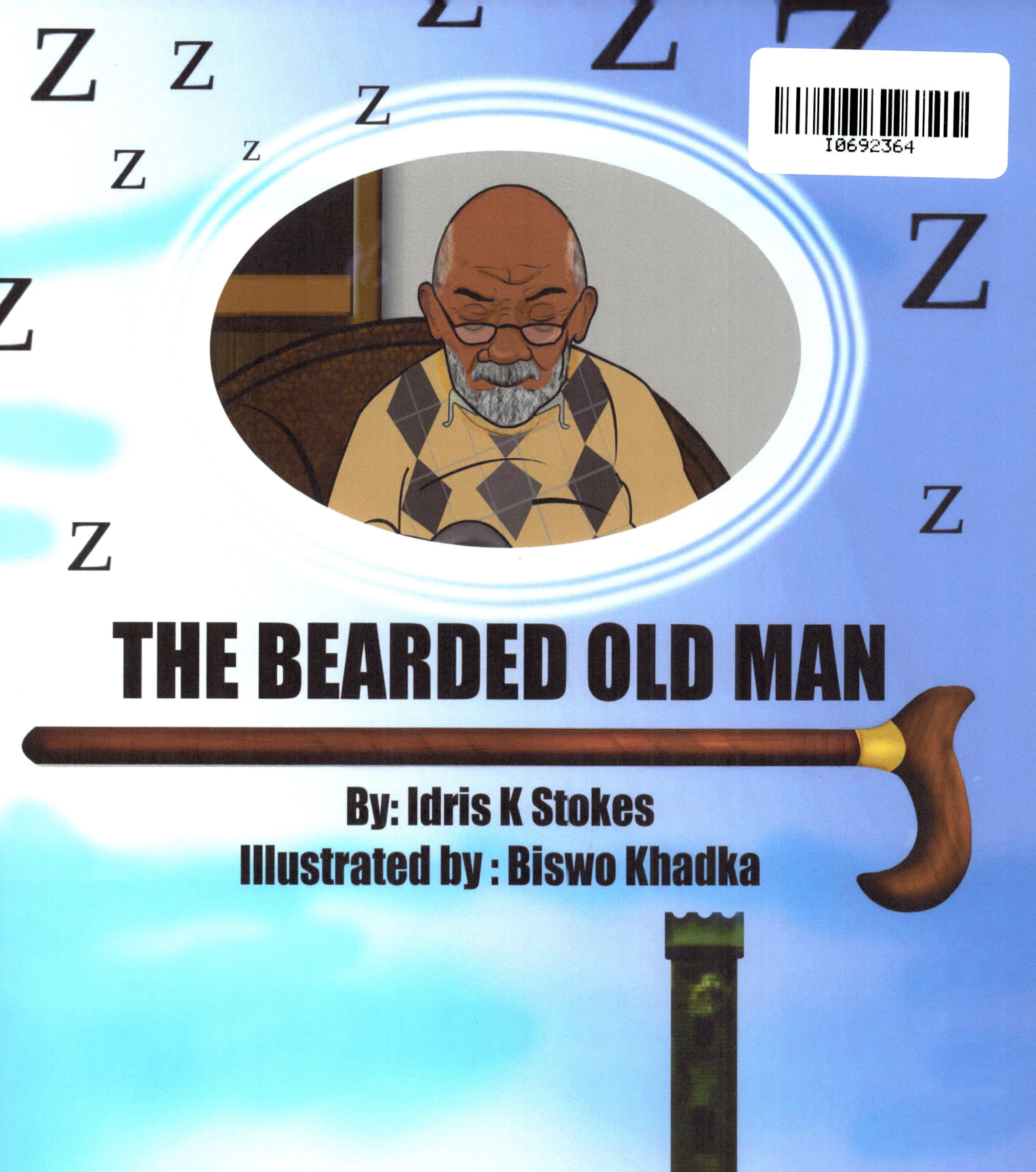

THE BEARDED OLD MAN

By: Idris K Stokes
Illustrated by : Biswo Khadka

The Bearded Old Man
Story by Idris K Stokes
Illustrated by Biswo Khadka

ISBN: 978-0-9987943-2-7
(Also available for Kindle)

Layout & prepress: Lighthouse24

There was a Bearded Old Man
who dreamt over and over again.
The Bearded Old Man was dreaming
about kids teasing him.

"Wake up, old man!
Wake up, old man!"
the old man's wife said to him.

"Your supper is ready
and you must eat!"
However, the Bearded Old Man
was quite in a deep sleep…

He was dreaming about jumping in a pool that was way too deep.

"You can't swim as fast as we can!" said the kids teasing the old man.

"Yes, I can! Yes, I can!"
said the Bearded Old Man.
"I'll show you kids
that I can swim."
as he stood at the edge
of the swimming pool,
afraid to jump in.

"We knew you couldn't swim!"
one little boy points to him.

So, the old man turns back around,
as the rest of the kids laughed at him.
All except this one little boy
who jumped in to swim.

That little boy's name was Tim.

The Bearded Old Man
starts to dream about
the kids teasing him again.

"Wake up, old man!
Wake up, old man!
You're dreaming again."
The old man's wife said to him.

"Your supper is ready
and you must eat.
Please old man
wake up from this sleep!"

But the Bearded Old Man's sleep
was just too deep....
He couldn't even think
to wake up and eat!

He then starts to dream about
kids teasing him at a track meet.

All the kids laughed at him,
except this one little boy they called Tim.

Tim ran fast and
beat all of them!

The old man then starts to dream
about these kids teasing him again.

"Wake up, old man!
Wake up, old man!"
the old man's wife
shakes him again.

Your supper is ready
and you must eat."
But the old man was still
in a deep sleep...

He didn't make a sound,
not even a peep.
He then began to dream
about sitting on a school bus's back seat.

"You can't go to school with us."
Now, the Bearded Old Man
was dreaming he was getting
on that yellow bus.

"They're not going to allow you
in our school.
You're too old, man.
You just wouldn't look cool."
said those kids who
continued to be rude.

"Yes, I can! Yes, I can!"
said the Bearded Old Man.

"I'll show you how cool
I'll be at school.
Let me on this bus!"
said the old man with a fuss.

But, the bus drove off,
leaving him in a dust.

All the kids laughed at him,
except this one little boy on that bus
who was waving his little hand
at the old man through the dust.

Is that... Is that him?
Yes, that little boy waving his hand was named Tim,
whom the Bearded Old Man
keeps dreaming about over and over again.

"Wake up, old man!
Wake up, old man!"
the old man's wife said
again and again.

"Your supper is ready
and you must eat."

The old man opened one eye,
and looked at his wife
to give her a peek.

But, he fully couldn't
wake up from his sleep to eat.
So, he closes his eye and starts to dream...
that he was joining a basketball team!

"You can't play
on our basketball team."
said one kid who
continued to be mean.

"You're not going to be able
to shoot the ball.
You need to be strong
and you're not tall anymore."
as one girl stretches
by the basketballs.

"Yes, I can! Yes, I can!"
said the Bearded Old Man.

"You just throw me that ball.
I'll show you I can shoot
and you don't have to be tall."

Suddenly,
as the bearded old,
fragile man
starts to shoot the ball,
he then realized
that he wasn't tall.

He hadn't swim
and couldn't run.
To finish school and play basketball
at his age didn't seem like much fun.

But, the Bearded Old Man
was great at all of these things
when he was young!

"I must wake from this dream...
What can they all mean?
Well, I guess I'm just a little old man
to these kids, so it seems."

The old man's wife stood over him
and shouted his name.
"Wake up, Tim!
Wake up, Tim!"
the Bearded Old Man's wife
says again and again.
"Your supper is ready
and you must eat."

The old man finally woke up to notice
this whole time he was asleep!

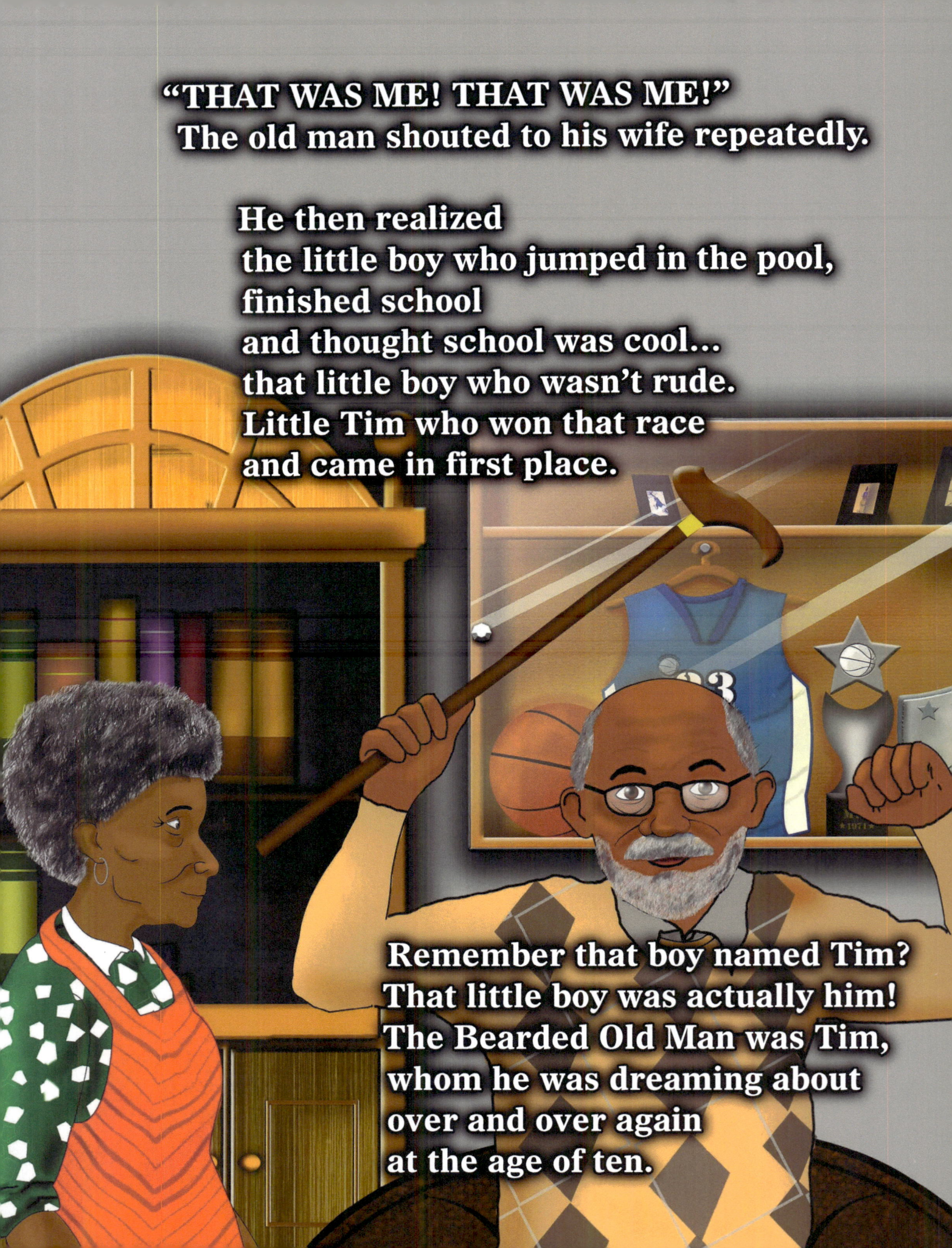

"THAT WAS ME! THAT WAS ME!"
The old man shouted to his wife repeatedly.

He then realized
the little boy who jumped in the pool,
finished school
and thought school was cool...
that little boy who wasn't rude.
Little Tim who won that race
and came in first place.

Remember that boy named Tim?
That little boy was actually him!
The Bearded Old Man was Tim,
whom he was dreaming about
over and over again
at the age of ten.

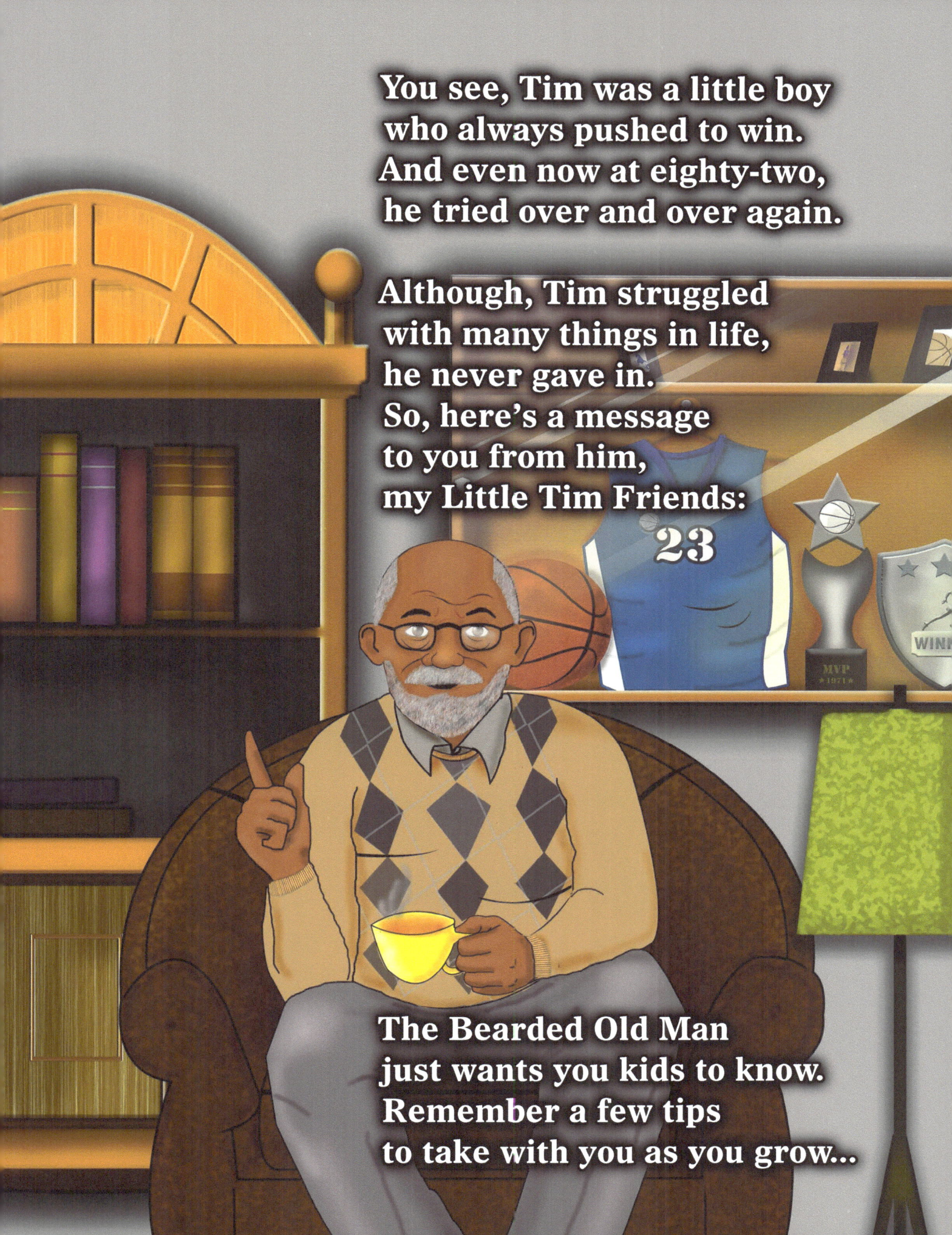

You see, Tim was a little boy
who always pushed to win.
And even now at eighty-two,
he tried over and over again.

Although, Tim struggled
with many things in life,
he never gave in.
So, here's a message
to you from him,
my Little Tim Friends:

The Bearded Old Man
just wants you kids to know.
Remember a few tips
to take with you as you grow...

Here's something to think about if you're mean,
and a few more tips to go along
with your big dreams:

- Always respect your elders
  and everybody in between.

- Never give up on yourself...
  Be nice not mean.

- Dreams come true,
  although, it might not seem!
  Keep going, keep going,
  you'll see what I mean.

- Stay young at heart,
  that's a way to be seen!
  And believe me, you will achieve anything
  if you follow your dreams!

I may be old,
   but I know many things.
      Listen to Grandpa Tim
         and you'll be sure to grow wings!!!

The End

www.ingramcontent.com/pod-product-compliance
Lightning Source LLC
Chambersburg PA
CBHW041545240626
47164CB00002B/132

* 9 7 8 0 9 9 8 7 9 4 3 2 7 *